Mehrdad Shahmoradi Mofrad has an artistic background. He studied in Vienna's Art School and attended some semesters at the Vienna's Film Academy as guest student and later as a part-time student for a year.

Mehrdad Shahmoradi Mofrad

ENDLESS MISSION

AUSTIN MACAULEY PUBLISHERS™

LONDON · CAMBRIDGE · NEW YORK · SHARJAH

A CIP catalogue record for this title is available from the British Library.

ISBN 9781528928410 (Paperback)
ISBN 9781528965477 (ePub e-book)

www.austinmacauley.com

First Published (2020)
Austin Macauley Publishers Ltd
25 Canada Square
Canary Wharf
London
E14 5LQ

Characters

Samuel Judd (Commander British Intelligence)
Henry Pinter (Commander British Intelligence)
Mrs Elisabeth Browning (James's Wife)
Mr James Browning (Colonel British Intelligence)
Miss Peggy Browning (James's sister)
Major John Barr (British Army Military)
General Paul Slyer
Henriette Bach (German spy)
Rudolf Schmidt (German spy, Henriette's fellow agent)
Wolfgang Schneider (German Spy in London)
Hans Benedict (German Scientist)
Two other German Scientists
Andreas Benedict (Hans Benedict's Cousin)
The Police Man

London and Berlin Scenes:
Unless otherwise: rainy
Night scenes: foggy

Scene 1

Henry Pinter is cutting a hole in a fence, which surrounds a garden, which surrounds a building.

He can now pass through the hole in the fence. He continues going towards the building.

He hears footsteps, which are coming towards him and hides behind a tall bush in the garden in front of the building.

A soldier is passing by the bush, Henry stands up; he takes one step away from the bush and beats the coming soldier on the head with the grip of his revolver.

The soldier falls unconscious on the ground, Henry takes the soldier's keys and goes towards the building next to where he is, unlocks the door and goes inside the building.

Scene 2

Inside the building,

In a room further down the corridor where two German soldiers are sitting, the red alarm lamp on the table begins to flash; they run out of the room.

Scene 3

In the corridor,

They see Henry Pinter who is standing further away in the corridor opposite them. He starts to shoot the two soldiers and can reach a laboratory and breaks the glass door into the laboratory.

The soldiers shoot him, he is injured. He throws his ID cards through the broken glass door into the laboratory in order to be destroyed and not to be found by the soldiers.

He pulls out a hand grenade, ignites it and throws it through the broken glass door to destroy the laboratory. The soldiers continue shooing till he falls on the floor.

Scene 4

Outside of the building,
A huge blast devastates the larger part of the building in which the laboratory was built.
The blaze and the dark smoke are rising higher and darkening the sky.

Scene 5

The camera focuses on British Military Intelligence Office.
Samuel enters the room where Major John Barr, his superior, is awaiting him.

SAMUEL:
Good morning, sir!

MAJOR BARR:
Please sit down. [*Pause.*] As far as we have been able to ascertain, the German army is experimenting with a toxic gas in the forest surrounding the northern part of Berlin.

A British doctor who used to work in a hospital in Berlin heard of some patients who had been hiking in the forest surrounding a factory and had showed symptoms of chemical gas after they had contact with it through breathing.

He reported this accident to us. He positively identified it as chlorine gas.

There must have been an explosion in the laboratory and the chlorine gas had leaked out of the laboratory. We presume that the laboratory has been repaired by now.

Samuel is listening and looking at the Major.

BARR:
He went to look for those patients who came in contact with this toxic gas. They described to him what the building looked like and where it was.

He drew some sketches after those descriptions.

There is a forester hut in some distance to it which is empty and not often checked.

Samuel, who is listening, asks:
It may be a good hiding place.

How about sending a commando to destroy the laboratory?

MAJOR BARR:
They will rebuild it. We need the scientists and their research results.

Another problem is that the German spies who are operating in London are concentrating more than before on our activities. We cannot risk sending such a group at present.

SAMUEL:
I understand, sir!

BARR:
You are a theatre actor, which will be a perfect cover for sending you to the Berlin Stadt Theatre as a guest actor.

You use the forester hut to coordinate your efforts.

You must look into how the building complex is secured.

After your penetration into the building and breaking into the laboratory, you collect some samples of the alleged chemical gas and other relevant documents which you might find relevant to it, if possible without drawing any attention.

He hands Samuel a German playbill with his cover (guest actor in the Berlin Stadt Theatre).

MAJOR BARR:
Do you have any questions?

SAMUEL:
No, sir!

MAJOR BARR:
Dismiss!

Scene 6

In James's Office,

JAMES:
I still insist that we should wait for Commander Pinter's return or to hear from him.

MAJOR BARR:
Pinter is overdue.

JAMES:
We do not know with certainty if Germans will definitely make military use of chlorine gas.

MAJOR BARR:
Yes, but we cannot take that risk.
Furthermore, the likelihood that what might have happened to Pinter may also happen to Judd is not negligible.
You did not tell him that Pinter is still missing and that the first mission might not have been carried out?

JAMES:
No, I did not tell him and indeed, it might be a risk.

After this, Major Barr looks at James silently.

Scene 7

Berlin, Germany.
Berlin Stadt Theatre,
Samuel is playing King Richard the Second in German.
King Richard:

Wo Worte selten, haben sie Gewicht.
(Where words are scarce, they are seldom spent in vain)
(King Richard the Second. Act II SCENE II)
Amongst the audience;
Henriette & Rudolf.

Scene 8

The play finishes.

Scene 9

Backstage, the camera follows Samuel to his dressing room, he goes inside.

Scene 10

Inside the dressing room
Samuel is sitting at the makeup table in front of the mirror and is removing his makeup.
He hears knocks on the door.

SAMUEL:
Kommen Sie bitte, herein.
(Come in, please.)

Henriette comes in the room and says:
Darf ich bitte, ein Autogramm haben?
(May I have an autograph?)
She hands a photograph of Samuel

SAMUEL:
Für wen darf ich schreiben?
(Whom should I write it to?)

HENRITTE:
Nein, bitte schreiben Sie die Fortsetzung;
(No, please continue the quotation)
"For they breathe truth that breathe their words in pain."
(King Richard the Second. Act II SCENE II)

Scene 11

Forest near Berlin, later on the same night;
Samuel is running towards the building complex; he approaches a bush near the fence which surrounds the main building. He turns his head to see if he is being followed and perceives a silhouette of an unknown person, but he is not certain of it.
He observes the guards. He finds it hard to go into the building from where he stands and leaves.

Scene 12

In the hotel,
Someone knocks on the door
SAMUEL:
Wer ist da?
(Who is there?)

Voice from outside,
Zimmer Service
(Room Service)
Samuel opens the door. Rudolf is standing at the door with drawn pistol.
Samuel quickly reacts and pulls him inside before Rudolf can trigger his pistol. He strikes Rudolf with a swift strike. Rudolf falls unconscious on the floor. Samuel searches Rudolf and finds his ID card: "Rudolf Schmidt", Deutsche Spionage Abwehr.
(German Counter Espionage)
He picks up the telephone on the table next to him and asks for his bill to be ready at once.

Scene 13

Next day
Deutsche Spionage Abwehr Building
Inside Rudolf's office;
Rudolf is telegraphing.

Scene 14

Somewhere in London,
Wolfgang Schneider is standing in a hotel room, holding a piece of paper and is reading it… After he has read it, he burns it.

Scene 15

SCENE cuts to late night in London.
Samuel is entering the Foreign Intelligence Building
Inside the building
He is going to see Major Barr
He enters his room, door closes. A conversation begins.

SAMUEL:
The guards, the fences, machine guns. Furthermore, I think that I was being followed.

BARR:
By whom?
SAMUEL:
I could not see.
MAJOR BARR:
He is looking at Samuel with a sad face and says:
You cannot use your cover. They are fully alerted by now and they assume that we want to destroy the lab.

We rather leave them in that assumption for the time being.

SAMUEL:
They will not give up.

MAJOR BARR:
Neither would I. They are trying to find a quicker way of mass murder. And I am trying to thwart them.

Major Barr remains silent and fearful holding his head with his hands.
After a while, Barr breaks the silence and says:

MAJOR BARR:
Can you think of an alternative plan?

Samuel remains without an answer.

BARR:
No, I suppose not.
Go and see Colonel Browning.

SAMUEL:
Sir!
He leaves the room.

Scene 16

At Browning's office,
These photographs are some of the new agents who we assume are working for German Intelligence. You might at some stage, during your mission, encounter them.

He shows him one particular photograph out of the rest.

JAMES:
Will she be a problem?

Samuel keeps his eyes locked on that photo.

SAMUEL:
Is she here in London?

JAMES:
She has been observed.

SAMUEL:
She was amongst the audience watching one of my appearances at the Berlin Stadt Theatre and came into the dressing room. She asked for an autograph. She was accompanied by one man; *and after short pause, he continues.*
There should be another way of carrying out this mission.

JAMES:
continues without a pause
We must construct a mask to avert the harmful effects of the chlorine gas.

SAMUEL:
It will be too late.

JAMES:
Now realises that there is something which Samuel is trying to form into words and asks:
What is troubling you, Samuel?

SAMUEL:
The war is raging across the continent. If we are going to stop the German's aggressions, we will need to work with them.

JAMES:
We have tried all the communication channels and so far, there hasn't been a response.

SAMUEL:
I am thinking of a new plan. Should we be successful, we will be able to convince the German Intelligence to recommend their government not to continue its aggression. But it requires deception. I will have to recruit German intelligence officers to provide me with information from the German Military in exchange for some quite trivial disinformation; nothing of any real value, and seemingly believable.

JAMES:
This has always been a moral challenge in our line of work. Will God forgive the lies that are for the greater good?

SAMUEL:
I can't reconcile the conviction that we need to work with them and the need to lie and deceive in order to prevent war.

JAMES:
You've been an intelligence officer alongside your acting career, are you not becoming idealistic?

SAMUEL:
I guess I am, sir! But let us, if only for a moment, assume that I will convince them of our cooperation.

James remains silent for a moment, looks Samuel in the eyes and says:

I let you move in that direction; however, you are to be aware of the consequences!

SAMUEL:
I will, sir!
(*Pause*) One of the Germans I have to recruit might be the woman who has been following my movements. She is in London. The woman on that photograph whom you enquired about.

JAMES:
How do you want to deceive her? You are puzzling me, Samuel; you have been under surveillance by her and maybe by some other German agents who are also in London.

SAMUEL:
She will come to see the opening of the new stage play.

JAMES:
Are you sure?

SAMUEL:
Yes.

JAMES:
Do you suspect she realises you work as an Intelligence Officer and are using your acting profession as your cover?

SAMUEL:
She probably knows it by now.

JAMES:
Have you informed Major Barr about your recruitment plans?

SAMUEL:
I would rather be certain of it before I inform the Major.

JAMES:
Dismiss!

SAMUEL:
Sir!

Samuel takes the file and the photo of the woman, stands up and leaves the room.

Scene 17

Later, at Samuel's house, outside the house at the kitchen back door. Wolfgang succeeds in unlocking the kitchen door.

Scene 18

He enters the house.
Inside the house
He goes up the stairs to go to the bedroom, before he reaches the last stair, Samuel opens the house door and sees Wolfgang.
Wolfgang draws his pistol and fires the first shot in Samuel's direction.
Samuel jumps out of Wolfgang's line of view and makes a sound as if he has been shot.

Samuel takes his revolver out of his Packet Jacket and waits for Wolfgang's next move.

Wolfgang goes down the stairs to see about Samuel; as soon as he reaches Samuel's vicinity, Samuel shoots Wolfgang and Wolfgang falls to the ground.

Samuel goes to the body which is lying on the ground in front of him and checks Wolfgang's pulse.

He goes to the telephone and dials a number; as soon as he hears a voice on the phone, he says:

Here is Commander Judd speaking, I need the cleaner at my home.

He looks at the body, walks towards it and starts searching the dead man's suit. He finds an ID of German Military Intelligence:

"Wolfgang Schneider"; Deutsche Ausland Intelligenze Offizier Sektion III (German Foreign Intelligence Officer Section III).

Scene 19

A sunny day
Long shot of the Foreign Intelligence Building, pedestrians are passing by and a woman with her back to the camera is in front of an easel, sketching.

Scene 20

Inside the building
Samuel, James and Barr are sitting at a table.

SAMUEL:
I have drawn the attention of the "Deutsche Spionage Abwehr".

BARR:
You have not been the only one.

SAMUEL:
What do you mean, not the only one?

JAMES:
We had sent Commander Pinter to destroy the laboratory and we have not heard from him since.
Samuel stands up and starts to walk around the room.

BARR:
Are you thinking of a possible cooperation with those on the photographs?

JAMES:
We took into consideration.

BARR:
Should we act on it?

JAMES:
I think it's our only option at present.

BARR:
We must offer them some information.

SAMUEL:
False information about some new weapons.

JAMES:
Our falsehood brings theirs back to us after a while.

BARR:
Yes, that is unavoidable, but we gain time.
SAMUEL:
Precious time to penetrate their organisation!

JAMES:
You are aware that you cannot any longer operate in Germany.

SAMUEL:
Yes, sir! It will not be necessary whilst two of their operatives are staying in London.
One is the woman on that photograph whose name is; "Henriette Bach". The other operative is "Rudolf Schmidt".

BARR:
Do you know them?

SAMUEL:
The woman came to my dressing room in Berlin Stadt Theatre and asked me for an autograph.
And the man tried to murder me in my hotel room.

Scene 21

Samuel walks out of the building in a distance to the woman who is still sketching.

Scene 22

Next day, Foreign Intelligence Building
In Samuel's office
Samuel is sitting at the table (facing the camera) and is marking some points on the maps according to the sketches described by the patients.
He stops, leans back in his chair and looks toward the window.
He stands up and goes,

Scene 23

Outside of the building
Samuel is standing in front of the woman and starts a conversation.

SAMUEL:
Do you want another autograph?

HENRIETTE:
Oh my God, it is you, Mr Judd? What a surprise!

SAMUEL:
A pleasant surprise I hope. "Henriette", isn't it?

Henriette smiles

SAMUEL continues:
What brings you to this part of London?

HENRIETTE:
I am visiting London and want to draw some sketches of
this building amongst many other places and buildings, which
are to follow.
(*Flirting a little*) I am just fascinated by the façade of this
building.

SAMUEL:
Really? You must be quite fascinated. I saw you looking
at those windows yesterday.

HENRIETTE:
Why? Do you work in that building?

SAMUEL:
Yes. May I invite you to tea?

HENRIETTE:
That would be nice; how may I call you, Mr Judd?
SAMUEL:
You may call me Samuel.
*Flash forward montage: SCENEs of Samuel and
Henriette walking up the street, having tea, apparently
walking in a park after holding hands, they appear to be*

getting more intimate; the montage closes with him kissing her goodnight. In her hotel room, three days later, they are lying in bed, obviously having had intimate relations.

HENRIETTE:
These last few days have been like a dream. I think I am falling in love with you.

SAMUEL:
I feel the same way.

HENRIETTE:
But I cannot continue without telling you the truth about me.

SAMUEL:
You had better keep your secrets to yourself. It will make you more mysterious and the others more inquisitive.

HENRIETTE:
Do you like mysteries and secrets?

SAMUEL:
I like secrets which can be unfolded without being harmful.
HENRIETTE:
How is secret to be defined?

SAMUEL:
In my experience, secrets are mostly negative and by times destructive after they will be revealed, for they remain unrevealed.

HENRIETTE:
In some occasions, revealing a secret will be a treason.

SAMUEL:
Not necessarily. I mean; one can trust another.

He kisses her.
HENRIETTE:
Can you imagine revealing yours?
I mean, do you work in that building?

SAMUEL:
Yes, I work there.
Henriette kisses him and asks him:
What are you?

SAMUEL:
I work as an intelligence officer, I know about you and your fellow agent.

Samuel pulls a file with her photo on an official paper.
Henriette takes the file and looks through the papers inside, remains calm (she is apparently embarrassed) and says:

Well, the best would be to discuss one another's complications.

SAMUEL:
I am offering you and your fellow agent cooperation. I want to know more about the lab in which the chemical gases are being produced.

HENRIETTE:
The laboratory is inside a building so much you already know.

SAMUEL:
How about the scientists?

HENRIETTE:
The scientists who work in the lab have been housed in the basement directly under it.

SAMUEL:
I still need both of you to accomplish a mission.

HENRIETTE:
What do you mean by a mission?

SAMUEL:
The only way to stop the development of the toxic gases is to take the scientists and the documents out of Germany.
I suggest that we all meet again in Hyde Park.

Henriette nods in agreement.

Scene 24

Samuel is on the stage and playing the role of Richard the second

Scene 25

Amongst the audience: James, Elisabeth and Peggy.

Scene 26

Not far from where they sit are also Henriette Rudolf are sitting.

Scene 27

Samuel is reciting:
SAMUEL:
'Nay. If I turn mine eyes upon myself, I find myself a traitor with the rest. For I have given here my soul's consent.'
(King Richard the Second Act IV SCENE 1, William Shakespeare's)

Scene 28

After a short while, he turns his eyes to Henriette and looks at her.

Scene 29

Henriette throws a flower for Samuel on the stage.

Scene 30

At the same time, Peggy's attention as well has been drawn to the woman who threw the flower to Samuel.
She looks at the woman and after some seconds at Samuel.

Scene 31

At the backstage
The curtain is down and players are leaving the stage.
Camera now follows Samuel's steps as he leaves the stage, walks towards the backstage and goes through the corridor in which he reaches his dressing room.

Scene 32

Samuel is cleaning his makeup in front of the makeup table's mirror as he hears knocking on the door.

SAMUEL:
Enter.

Scene 33

James, Elisabeth and Peggy walk in to the room. With mixed voices, they are simultaneously speaking with lines like those below:
'It was an astonishing performance; we enjoyed it.'
Whilst laughs are also audible.
JAMES:
I noticed your very intense voice during your acting.

SAMUEL:
(*Laughing*) I feared you would say that.

JAMES:
One.

SAMUEL:
Two.

JAMES:
'Truly the thing that I fear comes upon me.' (Job 3:25)

SAMUEL:
'And what I dread befalls me, I am not at ease, nor am I quiet.' (Job 3:25)

JAMES:
'I have no rest; but trouble comes.' (Job 3:26)

SAMUEL:
You are not only a good friend but also a good practice partner.

JAMES:
I know.

Samuel hands out a note to James.
James starts to read, the information about lab's locality, which Henriette gave.

ELISABETH:
Hurry, we want to celebrate.

PEGGY:
Yes, come on.

Scene 34

In a bar, after they leave the theatre; James, his wife Elisabeth, James's sister, Peggy, and Samuel are sitting together. They are drinking and chatting.
After a while, Samuel and Peggy stand up and go on the dance floor.

Elisabeth and James sitting alone at the table; an empty bottle of champagne is on the table and a half full one is in the ice bucket on the table.

Peggy and Samuel are dancing. Elisabeth is looking at Peggy and Samuel whilst those two are dancing.

ELISABETH (*looking at Peggy and Samuel*): They look happy together.

JAMES:
Yes, they like one another.

ELISABETH:
Do you think that they want to get married?

JAMES:
(*Realising her anxiety*) I cannot tell.

ELISABETH:
James, why not? You are Samuel's close friend. Aren't you curious?

James looks at her and smiles softly. Elisabeth is still looking at James awaiting an answer.

JAMES:
Your curiosity is enough for both of us.

ELISABETH:
Now, that's not an answer.
James looks at her softly and remains stubbornly silent. In the background: Peggy and Samuel are kissing one another whilst still dancing. Camera cuts to Samuel and Peggy.

SAMUEL:
I will be away for several weeks. Will you wait for me?

PEGGY:

I'll tell you when you come back.
They go back to the table.

Scene 35

At Samuel's flat. Samuel and Peggy are lying partially covered by a blanket, in bed, both sweating and hard breathing. After a while:

PEGGY:
Do you know that woman?

SAMUEL:
Which woman?

PEGGY:
The woman who threw a flower for you.

SAMUEL:
No.

PEGGY:
An unknown admirer?

SAMUEL:
Only one flower from the audience? Only one out of so many? The audience was pleased with my performance; wouldn't you agree?
He smiles and starts to whistle.

Scene 36

In Hyde Park, Samuel waits as Henriette and Rudolf approach. They begin to discuss. The camera pans in on the middle of the discussion.

SAMUEL:
Our clash in Berlin was unavoidable and regrettable, I do understand you.

Rudolf is looking at him indifferently.

SAMUEL:
We must work with one another to convince our governments that it will be best to negotiate and not to destroy and to kill. I am thinking of the use of chlorine gas by your military.

RUDOLF:
Are you accusing us of intending to use unconventional weaponry?

SAMUEL:
I am afraid, your military will be capable of using chlorine gas any time.
You knew about my attempt to spy on the laboratory; you followed me.

Rudolf remains silent and is looking at Henriette whilst listening to Samuel.

HENRIETTE:
Please, Rudolf; think of what we can achieve. We can save lives by stopping the production of the poisonous gases.

SAMUEL:
It will be preventive. We must stop the widening of the war and halt the usage of toxic gases.

RUDOLF:
is looking at Samuel.
How do you want to stop them? Do you want Henriette and me to go to them and order them to "STOP!"

SAMUEL:
I know that what I am asking you what appears to you to be unrealistic and by far impossible to achieve.

RUDOLF:
Tell us what you want from us.
SAMUEL:
I need both of you to go back to Germany and kidnap the scientists, who are developing the toxic gases, deliver them and the documents to us.

RUDOLF:
How long do you really know this man, Henriette?

HENRIETTE:
I suggest that we work with him.

RUDOLF:
What information will we receive from you?

SAMUEL:
I will offer you information about our weaponry.

RUDOLF:
What if this joint venture will not be justified as well minded intention but will be recognised as an act of treason?

SAMUEL:
Only time will tell.
Rudolf is still reluctant and draws a knife out of his jacket's pocket, points it towards Samuel and asks him:

RUDOLF:
How about "Wolfgang Schneider"? Did you also ask him to trust you and to work with you?

Henriette draws a small calibre revolver out of her bag.

SAMUEL:
I can explain.

Rudolf goes closer to Samuel.

Why did he have to be murdered?
SAMUEL:
He did not tell!
Rudolf points the knife at Samuel's throat.
Samuel does not move.

RUDOLF:
You are right, only time will tell.

Rudolf cuts Samuel's throat.
Samuel hold his hands on his throat and falls down on to the ground.
Henriette points the revolver towards Rudolf as Rudolf turns to Henriette with eyes wide open and raises his right hand in order to grab the revolver out of her hand; he takes one step towards her.
Henriette takes one step back and says:

I cannot trust you more than you can trust me.

Henriette shoots Rudolf in the forehead.
He drops down on the ground next to Samuel.
Henriette looks down at the two dead men lying on the ground.
The police arrive and place her under arrest.

Scene 37

Foreign Intelligence Building
Browning's office

BROWNING:
London is no longer a safe place to serve our purpose.

Barr, *who is listening, says:*
We must not contact our families nor our friends, we must keep silence.
JAMES:

Yes, I agree. They were the very German agents whom Judd intended to recruit.

We must move out of London and start to operate behind the German lines. We will use the same forester hut used by both Pinter and Judd, which is in a secure distance to the building complex.

BARR:
Don't you think that it will be under surveillance by now?

BROWNING:
We do not have another choice and are running out of time furthermore we must be sudden and with speed and we will start a new mission.

Barr nods in agreement.

JAMES:
We travel under cover of German travelling businessmen from London to Berlin; *Wir können Deutsch sprechen.*
(We speak German)

BARR:
Ja, Ich habe in der Schule das letzte Mal deutsch gesprochen.
(Last time I spoke German, I was in the school.)
I can understand but I cannot lead a conversation successfully.

JAMES:
I think that it will be adequate.

Scene 38

Forest outside Berlin, daylight;
It is raining, wind whistling, the ground is muddy.
A German soldier goes closer to the Forster hut. James and Barr are hiding in the storage room. He looks around the

hut. He looks through the window into the hut. He remains there a while standing and goes away.

Barr, who suspects that the soldier might have heard something and might call for support, goes out of the hut.

Scene 39

Outside the hut
He follows the soldier in some distance away from the hut, the soldier hears Barr's footsteps and turns and shoots Barr. Barr is wounded and shoots back at the soldier and kills him. He goes back to the hut and falls on the floor.

Scene 40

Inside the hut

BARR:
I have been shot at.

JAMES:
Let me see.

BARR:
Hold me up higher. It is my right arm.

JAMES:
Yes, I see the wound.
James looks into the wound and says;
The shot has only grasped your arm.
JAMES
Remains silent in front of the camera with Barr in the background as he tunes away from Barr.

JAMES:
As an actor, Samuel took the audience out of daily life by presenting them a parallel world to step in and to live in it for the duration of their stay in the theatre.

MAJOR BARR:
He is looking at James.
I never watched him on stage acting. I imagine acting with those two German agents as his supporting actor and actress…

He looks at James.
James is looking into plans on the table and listening to Barr.
Barr *continues:*

One of them was the better choice but the revengeful one blocked the entrance to the parallel world which Samuel created.
Should we enter it?

JAMES:
Looks at Barr and says:
I am afraid, that world does not exist any longer. It died with Samuel's murder. Furthermore, such a world will not last long to be trustworthy.

Barr coughs, takes a breath and starts to recite:
'Remember that my life is a breath, my eye will never again see well. The eye that beholds me will see me no more while your eyes are upon me… I shall be gone. As the cloud fades and vanishes. So those who go down to Sheol do not come up, they return no more to their houses, nor do their places know them anymore.' (*Job 7:7–10*)
JAMES:
Looks at Barr with astonishment and says:
One's breath poisons another man's breath.
Samuel's next stage appearance would have been playing the role of "Job".

BARR:
I would have been in the audience and watching him playing the role of "Job".

JAMES:
It will not be our place of death, "our sheol", not if we plan.

BARR:
It will not last long. They will find us here.

JAMES:
You are right. We have to act quickly.

BARR:
I am ready to proceed. I do not like unfinished tasks.

BROWNING:
Neither do I.

BARR:
What is your plan?
Browning looks at the plan of the building and says:
Look here; I noticed a fence which is for one minute unguarded.

BARR:
Do you think we can cut the wires in time and go into the building?

JAMES:
One of us ignites the dynamites and fires shots whilst the other one who is on the other side cuts the wires and goes into the building. He goes further down the stairs to the basement under the laboratory where the scientists are housed.
The cooperation with Henriette was not in vain.

BARR:
She gave valuable information.

JAMES:
Since we cannot kidnap the scientist, we will have to kill them and destroy the laboratory. Before they reinforce the guards, now that one of them is missing.
I'll arrange the distraction from that point.
He shows a point on the map.

BARR:
And I start from here and cut the wires of the fence on that point *(he is pointing at a location on the map)* and go into the building.
James concludes:
Let us start.
They pack the dynamites and they open the door, suddenly some shots are being fired at the hut from a distance.
They close the door, lower themselves and go to the only window in the hut.
They raise themselves high enough to be able to look out of the window.
They see masked German soldiers who are coming closer to the hut.
They break the window glass; start to shoot from inside the hut.

JAMES:
We must go out of the hut!
Ready?

BARR:
Ready.
James ignites two dynamites, opens the door and throws them out of the hut on the ground after the explosion.

Scene 41

Outside the hut
James and John come out of the hut and look around.
There is peace.

After a while, they start to march towards the building complex as suddenly an explosion, a mixture of smoke and chlorine gas surrounds them.

They disappear in it.

Scene 42

They are breathing hard and are not able to see properly through the masks.

As James falls over a dead German soldier, they find some others soldiers who are lying on the ground.

James and John take their gas masks immediately, wear them and change their own uniforms with the German soldiers' uniforms.

They are both exhausted and sit down on the ground for a while.

It is not long before they must stand up and hide themselves behind a tall bush as they hear footsteps and observe a number of masked German soldiers who are marching towards the forester hut and that they will eventually pass by their hideout.

As the last two German soldiers are close enough to the bush, James and John attack them, they fall on the ground.

James and John now are joining unobtrusively the rest of the soldiers who are still marching towards the hut.

After some minutes, they separate themselves from the rest, turn back, go towards the building and take off their masks.

They see a lorry which is going slowly towards the main entrance of the building complex.

They run after it and jump into the back of it.

Scene 43

In front of the gate
They reach the main gate.
After passing the main entrance gate at the back of the lorry, they jump out of the lorry.

After some minutes of walk inside compound, they are being spoken to.

A GERMAN SOLDIER:
Haben Sie sich verlaufen?
(Have you lost your way?)

JAMES:
Nein, wir sind neu und müssen zum Labor.
(No, we are new and must go to the lab.)

A GERMAN SOLDIER:
Gerade aus dann rechts abbiegen, das schwarze Gebäude.
(Straight forward then turn to the right, the black building.)
Ihre Ausweise und der schriftliche Befehl.
(Your prudentials and written order?)

JAMES:
Eine, Moment, bitte.
(Just moment.)

A GERMAN SOLDIER:
EINE, Moment?
(Just moment?)

JAMES:
Corrects: EINEN Moment, bitte!
(Just a moment, please.)

A GERMAN SOLDIER:
Woher kommt Ihr?
(Where do you come from?)

James turns to John, takes a knife out of his jacket, turns to the soldier, stabs him in his chest and takes the knife out.

They pull the dead soldier behind the wall of the gate's checkpoint.

They see two persons who are wearing white overalls and are walking through a narrow alley.

Scene 44

In the Alley
They follow them and can overpower them. They take their IDs and overalls and go towards the black building. They pass through the entrance of the black building and go inside.

Scene 45

Inside the building
They are standing in front of a very large and long corridor with doors on both sides.
It is a crowded corridor.
Staff walk across it, some personnel who are standing and speaking with one another and other personnel who come out and some who go into the offices.
The corridor leads into another building which is separated by a glass door on which there is a shield.

"Haupt Labor"
(Main Laboratory)

JAMES:
Whispers.
We must speak German, just follow me, we must go through that glass door.

James speaks Lauder in German:
Wir müssen bessere Ergebnisse erzielen!
(We must achieve better results.)

JOHN:
Ja!

(Yes)

They reach the glass door and go inside.
They approach the spot where Henry Pinter was killed and the explosion had occurred.
They pass by it, find their way to the stairway which leads down to the scientist's accommodations in the basement. They go down.

Scene 46

They are now in the basement, they see a door next to where the beds are situated; John opens it. It is a storage room, they go inside it and close the door.
After an hour, some personnel come in the room.
James opens the door and they come out of the room.
Slowly, they approach the accommodation room where the personnel are changing their clothes.

JAMES:
Keine bewegt sich!
(No one moves.) *With a revolver in his right hand.*

ONE OF THE PERSONNEL:
Was wollen Sie?
(What do you want?)

JAMES:
Wer von Ihnen ist der Ober Wissenschaftler?
(Which one of you is the head scientist?)

THE SAME PERSONNEL:
Keine von uns.
(None of us.)

JAMES:
Wo ist er?
(Where is he?)

THE SAME PERSONNEL:
Sie leben nicht hier. Sie werden jeden Tag hier gebracht. Wir wissen nicht wo sie leben.
(They do not live here. They are brought here every day. We don't know where they live.)
Was wollen Sie von ihnen?
(What do you want from them?)

JOHN:
What is he answering?

JAMES:
The head scientists do not live here.

JOHN:
What shall we do now?

JAMES:
We take the documents.
Wo sind die chlorine Gas Dokumente?
(Where are the documents about the chlorine gas?)

THE SAME PERSONNEL:
You are spies, English spies, aren't you? Are you looking for the one who came here?

JAMES:
In a way. What did happen to him, were you here at the time?

THE SAME PERSONNEL:
Yes, I was here. The guards shot him but before he was dying on his injuries, he was able to pull out a hand grenade and ignite it.
He blew up the guards and himself, but not the laboratory.

JOHN:
I don't trust what he is telling us.

JAMES:
Neither do I. I think that he is keeping us busy here.
Lay down on the floor all of you with your hands behind your heads!
John, you tie their hands with those cloths on that table there.

John does as James asked him to do and after he is finished, he says:

We must blow the laboratory; it'll stops them for a while.

THE SAME PERSONNEL:
Whilst lying on the floor with his hands on his head, says:

It will not damage much. The laboratory is secured with solid metal walls.
The glass door which you probably saw is only the first entry and after that, the metal entry door is installed.

JAMES:
You all can stand up and be at ease.
John untie their hands, please!

He asks the same personnel
Do you have suggestions?
THE SAME PERSONNEL:
All of us whom you can see here, have seen the repercussions of the chlorine gas during the dreadful scientific experiments on the experimental rabbits.

John interrupts him and says to James:
We are not here to start trusting him, not after what happened to Judd.

The same personnel continues:
The military has decided on using it as a part of its weaponry.

We are in discomfort with these developments which go behind the usage of conventional weaponry.

JAMES:
I think that we should trust him for there is not another option. Let us hope that we are luckier than Judd.

THE SAME PERSONNEL:
Look here, I have kept Henry Pinter's ID cards. They survived the blast because of the security measures which I mentioned before. I found them in the laboratory after the blast as we started to clean the lab and did not show them to anyone.

John *asks him:*
What is your name?

THE SAME PERSONNEL:
My name is Hans Benedict.

JAMES:
Hans, do you intend to help us to put a halt to the further production and use of the gases, which are being produced here?

HANS:
Yes, but as you observe, everything is so perfectly planned and secured that there isn't a possibility of going into the laboratory let alone to destroy it.

JAMES:
I know now.

JOHN:
How about the rest of your colleagues? Are they also willing to cooperate?
Hans looks at them and they nod in agreement.
One of them takes some steps forward and says:

We can give you the formulas which will enable your scientists to design a mask to filter out the chlorine gas. I have a cousin in Liverpool whom you can also contact, I'll write you the address.

James and John look and smile at one another and shake hands with Hans.

HANS:
We will help you to get out of the building early tomorrow morning. You better go back to the storage room for the night.

Scene 47

MoD Building London
Office of General Slyer
James and John are sitting on the general's table. As the general comes into the room, they stand up. The general goes to his chair, sits down and says:

Take your seats, gentlemen.
I congratulate you on your accomplishment.

JAMES:
Thank you, sir!

JOHN:
Thank you, sir!

GENERAL:
We did not have an open communication line with you, for in London the enemy agents were practically everywhere and we could not risk to let them know about your movements.
Your plan was brilliant, I must say.
The formulas which you have brought with you are genuine.
We have now the mask to protect the soldiers but we had to develop our own chlorine gas to test the mask of their

averting potentiality before you returned from the field. Nevertheless, I deeply express my gratitude and ask for your understanding.

John and James look at one another and then at General Slyer.

JAMES:
May I ask you, sir; if the British army will use toxic gases as weapons?

GENERAL SLYER:
I cannot tell.
Some silent seconds!
Dismiss!

JAMES:
Sir!

JOHN:
Sir!
James and John stand up and leave the general's office.

Scene 48

John and James are walking on the Thames promenade. Restlessly exhausted, they sit down on a bench.
Some time passes.

JOHN:
The world is becoming more unpredictable.

JAMES:
I do not remember it to have been helpfully predictable except in our profession.
It contradicts our profession not to be foreshadowing.
Unless a spy becomes romantically idealistic.
I am sure that Samuel experienced it intensively, certainly more than we ever shall.

JOHN:

Yes, realism is the essential part of human decency.

I gather that you are trying to tell me something.

JAMES:

Yes, something which is hidden deep within one's innermost. I cannot find its whereabouts nor find a name for its place.

JOHN:

Indeed, neither can. I suggest we pay a visit to look up Hans Benedict's cousin in Liverpool.

JAMES:

We travel by train early tomorrow morning.

We aimed at destroying the toxic gases productions and their formulas in Germany.

Now we are confronting our own army's possible usage of the poisonous gases against the enemy.

They will not halt there and they will develop even deadlier ones.

JOHN:

And we cannot stop our own military… That will be treason…

JAMES:

But we can stop the Germans. By doing so, our military will not have reasons to pursuit the usage the chemical gas warfare as retaliations.

JOHN:

It is an endless mission and it is becoming an arm's race.

Scene 49

At the house of Andreas Benedict

John and James are sitting in living room and are being served with tea and biscuits.

ANDREAS:
Hans, my dear cousin, sends you. How did you get to know him?

JAMES:
We had a trading business in Germany.

ANDREAS:
A business in the middle of the war?

JOHN:
Yes, we are businessmen.

ANDREAS:
I see.

JAMES:
We import and export.

ANDREAS:
What brings you to me?

JOHN:
We wonder if you could contact your cousin, since we have difficulties of finding him, you know the war…

ANDREAS:
And what in particular should I tell him from you?

JAMES:
Yes, you can tell him from us that since our last meeting things conditions of business have changed quite drastically on our part as well as on his.

JOHN:

And that we would like him to inform us about new developments which are being achieved.

ANDREAS:
He will certainly know what you mean by it?

JOHN:
Oh, yes!

ANDREAS:
How can I pass his message to you, should there be one?

JOHN:
Good question, here is my card.
James is looking at the garden in front of the living room says:
You have a beautiful garden.

ANDREAS:
Gardening is a hobby of mine.

JOHN:
Well, thank you for the tea and the biscuits.
James and John leave the house.

Scene 50

Outside the house
They walk away from the house

JAMES:
We will ask the next police station about the; "Andreas Benedict", I have a feeling…

JOHN:
Your instinct? You forgot your bag in the living room.

JAMES:
One of the things which grows with one as one gets older. How about yours?

JOHN:
I do not deny that I have some. I think that he wanted to tell us something.

JAMES:
Yes, so do I.

Scene 51

At the police station
James and John show the police on duty desk their prudentials

JAMES:
We require information about a German decedent by the name of "Andreas Benedict", he is a medical doctor.

POLICEMAN:
Looks through the registration cards for foreigners, finds his card and says:
The registration has been filled in correctly.

JOHN:
Any next of kin?

POLICEMAN:
He hasn't any next of kin in England but in Germany, the given name is; "Hans Benedict", a cousin of his.
James and John leave the police station.

Scene 52

Outside of the police station, they are standing. John says:
He seems to be what he is.

JAMES:
Let us stay in Liverpool for a while and observe him. I'll start the surveillance.

JOHN:
I replace you in three hours.

James finds a safe place in a distance to Andreas' house.
As it gets darker, a car drives to the house stops, a man and a woman get out of the car whilst the driver remains in the car seated.
After about an hour, they come out, get into the car and they drive away.
James goes to the house and knocks on the door. Andreas opens the door.
James *says:*
I am sorry to impose on you. I think I forgot my bag in the living room.

ANDREAS:
Wait here. I'll get it for you.

JAMES:
You are a spy, aren't you?

ANDREAS:
What, a spy?

JAMES:
Yes.

ANDREAS:
I'll get your bag.
He walks away from the door and goes towards the living room and says loudly:
A spy! No, I am not. But I suppose that you are one.
JAMES:
Yes, I am.

ANDREAS:
Do come in.

JAMES:
We need help. It is a matter of most urgency.

ANDREAS:
Is it about chemical warfare?

JAMES:
Correct. On which side are you?

ANDREAS:
I cannot think of using mass murder weapons. That is behind humanity.

JAMES:
What did those persons want with you?

ANDREAS:
They are German spies who keep an eye on me because of my cousin. Your visit here today drew their attention.

JAMES:
What did you tell them?

ANDREAS:
Just that you wanted to sell me some books.

JAMES:
Can you send our message to Hans after all?
ANDREAS:
Yes.
James leaves the house and meets John who is waiting outside. He tells him about his conversation with Andreas along the way to the railway station.

Scene 53

London at John's flat
James and John are sitting at the table and having dinner together.

JOHN:
The man and the woman are worrying me. We do not know what they had discussed with Andreas.

JAMES:
It could have been anything. You gave Andreas this address?

JOHN:
Yes, is something troubling you?

JAMES:
It is the revolver, which is lying openly on your desk.

JOHN:
Oh that revolver, I always keep it loaded for not to forget that I am a secret agent. Let us try this wine.

JAMES:
A Riesling!

JOHN:
I have kept this bottle for a long time.
At the same time, a loud sound draws their attention to the entrance door as the man and the woman, previous observed by James, break into the flat and start to shoot with their pistols, which are equipped with silencers towards John and James.
John takes hastily his revolver, which lies on the small desk next to the table and can shoot the man.
The woman shoots James in the head and James falls from his chair on the floor.

John who had jumped from his chair after he shot the man aims the revolver to the woman and shoots her several times at her chest and she falls on the floor.

John stands up from behind the table, goes towards the dead James, stands still by him.

He takes one step towards the telephone on the table, picks up the receiver and dials a number.

He hears a voice on the other side of the line and says:

Here is Major Barr speaking; I need the cleaner at my flat.

He puts the receiver back on the telephone and suddenly he feels cold in his left leg.

He stretches his right hand and reaches the wounded point as he realises that he has been shot at his left leg. The bloodstains on his hand ascertain him of it that he is slowly bleeding.

He feels pain but still standing, he takes some steps towards the window in front of him, he stands before it and looks at the landscape outside the window, which is covered by thick cloud of fog.

It is reminding him of the scenes from his mission which were covered with chlorine gas and he had left behind. And now he is again confronted with its consequences.

He whispers:

Will this mission ever end?

The End